Bow-Wow's
Nightmare
Neighbors

Mark Newgarden & Megan Montague Cash

A Neal Porter Book
Roaring Brook Press
New York

01-27-15

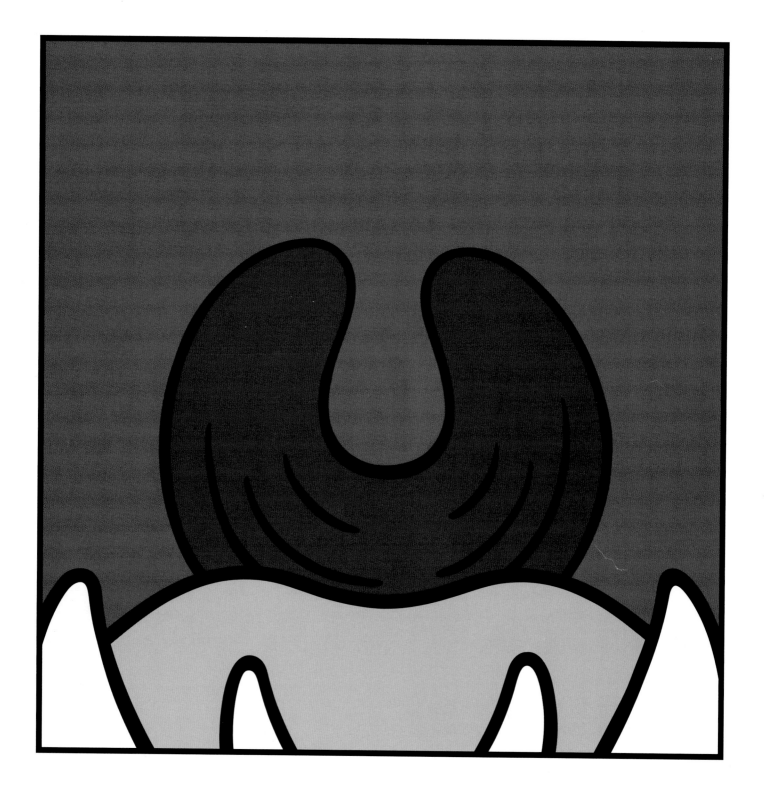

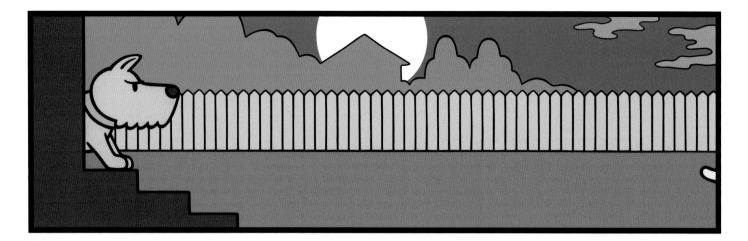

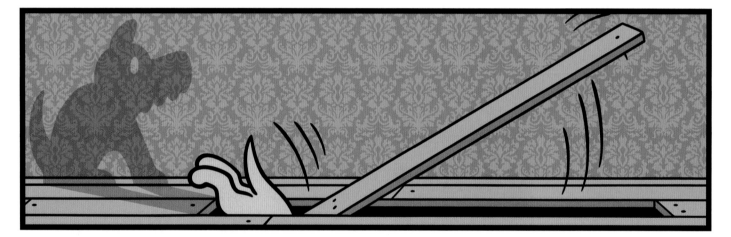

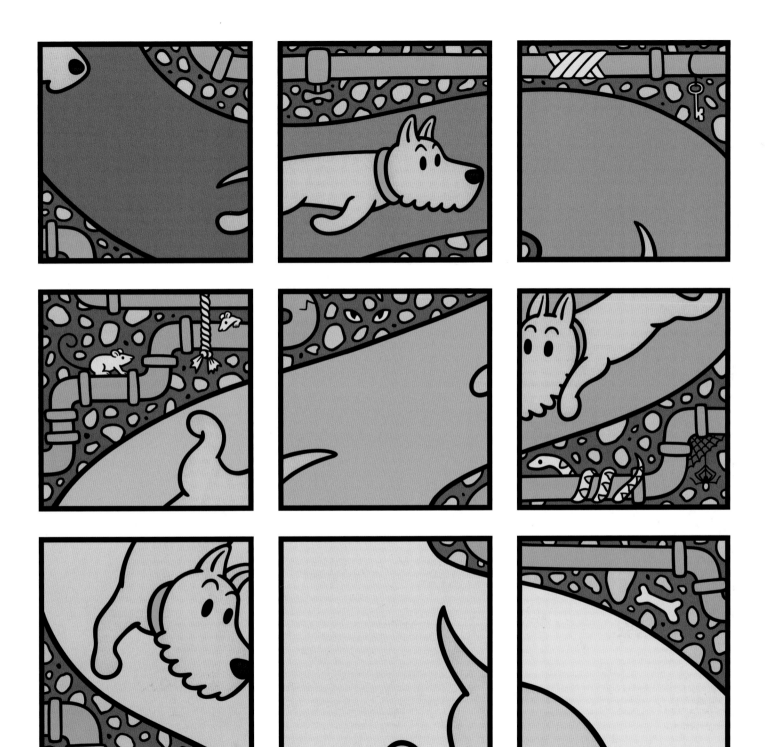

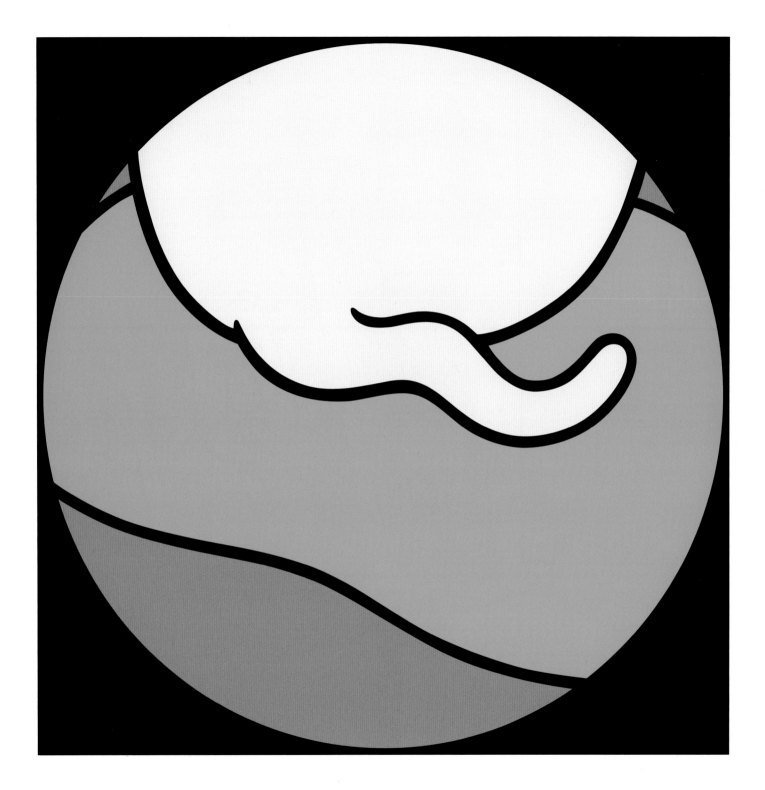

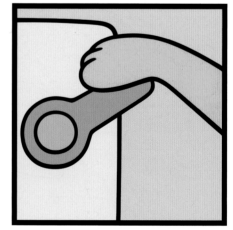

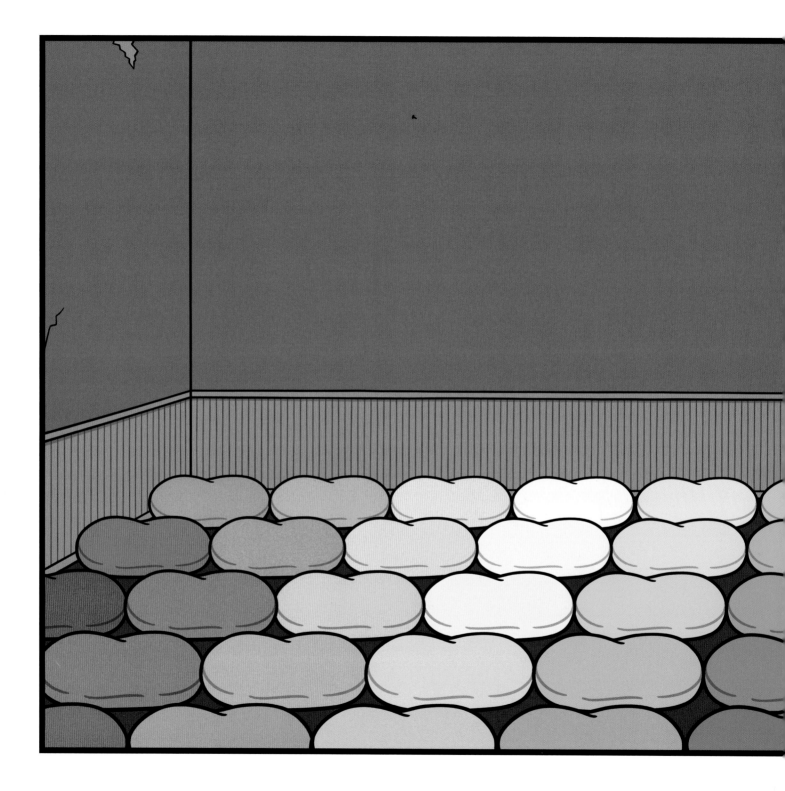

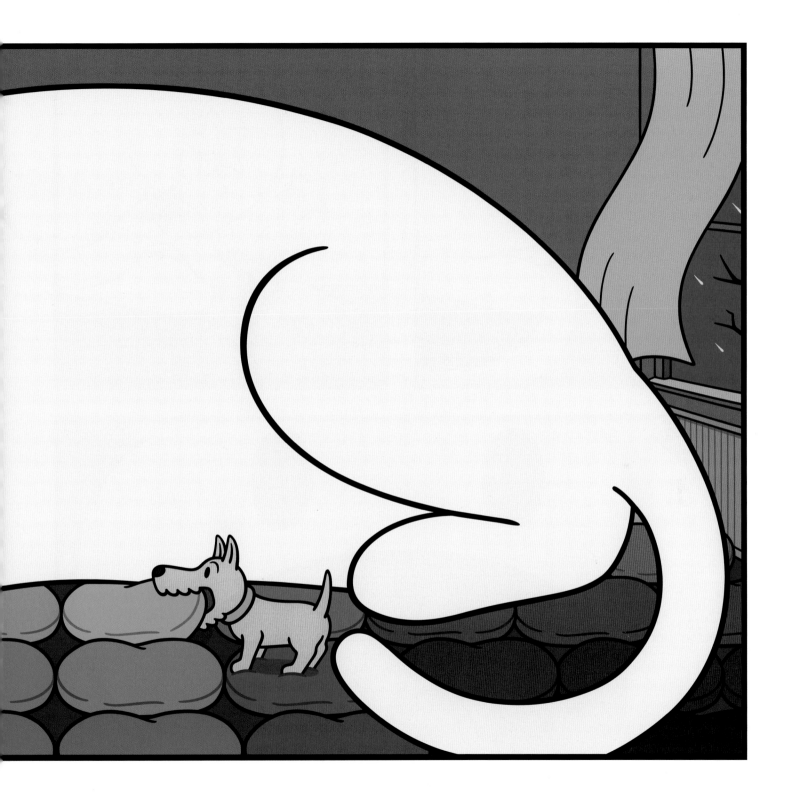

(Well, there had to be *some* words.)

Copyright © 2014
by Mark Newgarden & Megan Montague Cash
A Neal Porter Book / Published by Roaring Brook Press
Roaring Brook Press is a division of
Holtzbrinck Publishing Holdings Limited Partnership
175 Fifth Avenue, New York, New York 10010
mackids.com All rights reserved

Library of Congress Cataloging-in-Publication Data

Newgarden, Mark.
Bow-Wow's nightmare neighbors / Mark Newgarden,
Megan Montague Cash. — First edition.
pages cm
Summary: "Bow-Wow, an expressive dog, tangles with
some unruly neighbors in this wordless, spooky Halloween
picturebook"— Provided by publisher.
ISBN 978-1-59643-640-4 (hardcover)
[1. Dogs—Fiction. 2. Halloween—Fiction. 3. Neighbors—
Fiction. 4. Stories without words.]
I. Cash, Megan Montague. II. Title.
PZ7.N4793Bv 2014
[E]—dc23

Roaring Brook Press books may be purchased
for business or promotional use.
For information on bulk purchases please contact
Macmillan Corporate and Premium Sales Department at
(800) 221-7945 x5442
or by email at specialmarkets@macmillan.com.

First edition 2014
Book design by Megan Montague Cash
Printed in China by Toppan Leefung Printing Ltd.,
Dongguan City, Guangdong Province

1 3 5 7 9 10 8 6 4 2